THE CAT ON THE DOVREFELL

THE CAT ON THE DOVREFELL

A Christmas Tale

Translated from the Norse by
SIR GEORGE WEBBE DASENT

illustrated by Tomie de Paola

G.P. Putnam's Sons • New York

With special thanks to Peggy Coughlan,
for her wise and generous advice.

Illustrations copyright © 1979 by Tomie de Paola
All rights reserved. Published simultaneously in Canada
by Longman Canada Limited, Toronto.
Printed in the United States of America

LIBRARY OF CONGRESS CATALOGING IN PUBLICATION DATA
Main entry under title:
The Cat on the Dovrefell.
Translation of Kjetta på Dovre from Norske folke-
eventyr, collected by P. C. Asbjørnsen and J. Moe.
SUMMARY: The trolls pay Halvor an annual Christmas
visit until they encounter a great white cat.
[1. Folklore—Norway. 2. Christmas stories]
I. Dasent, George Webbe, Sir, 1817–1896. · II. De Paola,
Thomas Anthony.
PZ8.1.C2295   398.2'1'09489   [E]   78-26340
ISBN 0-399-20680-9
ISBN 0-399-20685-X pbk.

Once on a time there was a man up in Finnmark who had caught a great white bear, which he was going to take to the King of Denmark.

Now, it so fell out, that he came to the Dovrefell just about Christmas Eve, and there he turned into a cottage where a man lived, whose name was Halvor, and asked the man if he could get houseroom there, for his bear and himself.

"Heaven never help me, if what I say isn't true!" said the man. "But we can't give anyone houseroom just now, for every Christmas Eve such a pack of trolls come down upon us that we are forced to flit, and haven't so much as a house over our own heads, to say nothing of lending one to anyone else."

"Oh!" said the man, "if that's all, you can very well lend me your house! My bear can lie under the stove yonder, and I can sleep in the side-room."

Well, he begged so hard, that at last he got
leave to stay there. So the people of the house
flitted out, and before they went, everything was
got ready for the trolls.

The tables were laid, and there was rice porridge, and fish boiled in lye, and sausages, and all else that was good, just as for any other grand feast.

So, when everything was ready, down came the trolls. Some were great and some were small; some had long tails and some had no tails at all; some, too, had long, long noses.

And they ate and drank, and tasted everything.

Just then, one of the little trolls caught sight of the white bear, who lay under the stove.

So he took a piece of sausage and stuck it on a fork, and went and poked it up against the bear's nose, screaming out:

"Pussy, will you have some sausage?"

Then the white bear rose up and growled, and hunted the whole pack of them out-of-doors, both great and small.

Next year Halvor was out in the wood, on the afternoon of Christmas Eve, cutting wood before the holidays, for he thought the trolls would come again.

And just as he was hard at work, he heard a voice in the wood calling out:
"Halvor, Halvor!"
"Well," said Halvor, "here I am."
"Have you got your big cat with you still?"

"Yes, that I have," said Halvor. "She's lying at home under the stove, and what's more, she has now got seven kittens, far bigger and fiercer than she is herself."

"Oh, then, we'll never come to see you again," bawled out the troll away in the wood. And he kept his word, for since that time the trolls have never eaten their Christmas brose with Halvor on the Dovrefell.